This book is for:

_____

The Very Best Grandfather in the Universe

according to me:

_____

To Jeffrey Steinberg, the world's greatest "Daba"—DJS

To my wonderful Grandpa John, the best grandpa I could have asked for, and who will always be cherished and loved—RH

GROSSET & DUNLAP
An imprint of Penguin Random House LLC, New York

First published in the United States of America by Grosset & Dunlap,
an imprint of Penguin Random House LLC, New York, 2022

Text copyright © 2022 by D. J. Steinberg
Illustrations copyright © 2022 by Ruth Hammond

GROSSET & DUNLAP is a registered trademark of Penguin Random House LLC.

Visit us online at penguinrandomhouse.com.

Library of Congress Cataloging-in-Publication Data is available.

Manufactured in China

ISBN 9780593387115

10 9 8 7 6 5 4 3 2 1 HH

MY GRANDPA IS THE BEST!

BY
D. J. STEINBERG

ILLUSTRATED BY
RUTH HAMMOND

GROSSET & DUNLAP

Mount Grandpa

It's fun to climb Mount Grandpa.
I climb right to the top,
then flip myself back over
with a twirl and a flop!
Then up again and down again
and all around the mount again
until Mount Grandpa's had enough,
and then we both go *plop!*

S-P-E-L-L-I-N-G W-H-I-Z

My grandpa told the waiter
and the lady at the store
and the mailman and the pizza guy
who came to the front door.
I guess that Grandpa must be proud
of my last spelling quiz—
he's telling all the world that
his granddaughter is a whiz!

Time for Tea

Pop-Pop, come—it's time for tea!
I poured a cup for you and me,
and all my dolls, and Teddy, too.
Now all we're waiting for is YOU!

Time Travel Kisses

Do Grandma and Grandpa come from the future?
They live so far away
that when it's *our* morning,
we send kisses good night
'cause for *them* it's the end of their day!

Again and Again and Again!

My grandpa reads my favorite book
from cover to cover and then
I ask him to start at the very first page
and read it all over again!

The Scream Machine

I squeeze my grandpa's hand as the cars clank
    up the track.
Then *creak-creak-creak* we start downhill.
Oh no—I'm scared . . . "Go back!"
But Grandpa holds me tight: "Just close your
    eyes and count to ten."
And like that, the ride is over . . .
That was it? "Let's go again!"

Ice-Cream Dream

I've dreamed a thousand dreams
of the *Mega Yum Supreme*
with all the toppings that they serve
at Archibald's Ice Cream.
And today my grandpa ordered one!
It sure is *mega-yummy.*
But it's also *mega-WAY-TOO-BIG*
to fit inside my tummy!

Leader of the Pack

My grandfather loves to go hiking.
He always leads the pack
and shouts, "Come on, you slowpokes!"
as we huff and puff in back!

My Gramps Can Dance!

Gramps puts on a record,
and his feet begin to move.
He shuffles, shakes, and shimmies
as he gets into the groove,
and before I even know it,
he takes me by my wrist,
and I giggle as we wiggle
to a dance he calls "the Twist"!

★ ♦ ★ ♥ ★

Pick a Card

Pick a card, any card . . . which card did you pick?
Could it be *this* one? I know Grandpa's trick!
Bet *you* want to know how to do it as well.
So sorry, but magicians like us never tell!

Dig-Dig-Digging

It's time for spring! Which means one thing—
my grandpa's pulling weeds.
We help him dig-dig-dig the dirt
to plant some veggie seeds.
Now push them deep down in the soil—
we plant them row by row
and sprinkle them with water
as we shout out, "Grow! Grow! Grow!"

Cucumber Emergency!

Those seeds were sure good listeners.
They grew and grew and grew,
till Grandpa called today and said,
"Come pronto—I need you!"
We helped him pick the cucumbers
and put them on a plate—
and then we all deserved a snack,
so guess what we all ate?

Cannonball!

When Grandpa steps up to the pool—
take cover! Better dash!
'Cause a cannonball is coming
with a giant Grandpa **splash**!

So Many Names

There are Peepaws and Pop-Pops, Grand-Pères
  and Papas,
Zaydas and Nonnos and Lolos and Boppas.
Some gramps are called Opa, Abuelo, Papou . . .

. . . but the best name of all is the one I call you!